To Christopher,

You never know
what you can do
till you try.

William Crain
12/25/01

The Whistling Frog

from
Lily Pad Pond

Written by William Crain

Illustrated by Brian Crain

Littlest Lamb Publishing
Coeur d'Alene

To my grandmother, Ollie Belle Taylor—
And my granddaughter, Jamie Rome Crain—
The unbroken chain.

And to the little boat guy,
Whose sail is just over the horizon.

littlestlamb.com

Text copyright © 2001 William Crain
Illustrations copyright © 2001 Brian Crain

First edition

ISBN: 0-9705483-9-7
Library of Congress Card Number: 00-192581

I'll tell you a story—
I know that it's true—
Of a little green frog
And what he could do.

That *sad* little frog
From Lily Pad Pond
Lived over the hill
And a little beyond.

He was very unhappy.
When he tried to go *croak*,
All the other frogs laughed
That his croaker was broke.

He would take a **deep** breath

And try to **croak croak,**

But out came **tweet tweet,**

Like a little bird spoke. _tweet_

Frog lowered his head,
And he sniffed and he sighed,
"I'm a frog who can't croak."
Then he sat down and cried.

"Oh, why am I here
On Lily Pad Pond?
Why not on the hill?
Or why not beyond?"

"I can teach you to **m o o**,"
Said the little bull calf.

But the little duck quacked,
"Please, **don't** make me laugh."

"Whoever heard
Of a frog who could **moo**?
So what if he could,
What good would it do?"

"You should learn how to **quack**.
Now that's a good trick.
You could quack just like me

QUACK

When you *slip* where it's *slick*."

So Frog mooed a weak moo,
And he quacked a weak quack.
Then he tried to croak croak,
And the sadness came back.

Sniff, sniff. Little frog sniffs.
Sigh, sigh. Little frog sighs.
He wiped away tears
From his little frog eyes.

"Oh, Lily, my lily pad,
What can I do?
Duck wants me to quack.
Calf wants me to moo."

"I *don't* want to sound
Like a **duck** or a **cow**.
I'm a **frog**. I should **croak**.
But I just don't know how."

"What can I do, Lily?
Where can I go?"
But lily pads don't
Answer back, as you know.

And the mood *spread* like ripples
On Lily Pad Pond.
It *spread* to the hill
And on toward beyond.

It was just then a wind came
And started *to* blow.

It blew HARDER and **HARDER**,
And wouldn't *you* know—

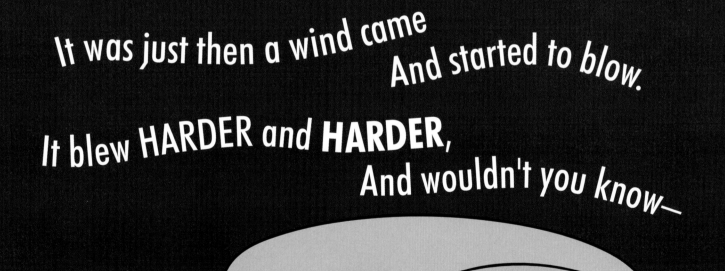

That wind blew the lily pad
To the top of the hill,
With the little green frog
Hanging onto it still.

Then it suddenly stopped!
And before Frog could think,
He dropped **PLOP!**
In a birdbath
Where birds come to drink.

There were redbirds and blackbirds
And birds that were blue,
And a boy on a bike,
And a dog and cat, too.

"Who are **you**?" said the boy.

Frog wanted to croak,
But he *tweeted* instead,
Like a little bird spoke.

"What if stars could not twinkle and shimmer and shine?

That's a **very** sad story,

but not sad as mine."

"This," said the boy,
"Is the very first time
I've heard a frog speak
About stars, **and in rhyme**!"

Frog took a deep breath,

Then from deep down inside
Came another sweet **tweet**!

And he sat down and cried.

"But why are you sad?"
Said the dog and the cat.

"I'm a frog who can't croak.
What is **sadder** than that?"

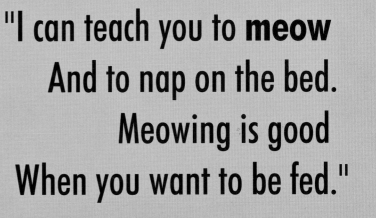

"I can teach you to **meow**
And to nap on the bed.
Meowing is good
When you want to be fed."

"I can teach you to **bark**.
When the cat comes to play,
You could bark at it **loud**
And chase it away."

"No, thank you." Frog sniffed.
"I should croak like a frog,
 Not meow like a cat
 Or bark like a dog."

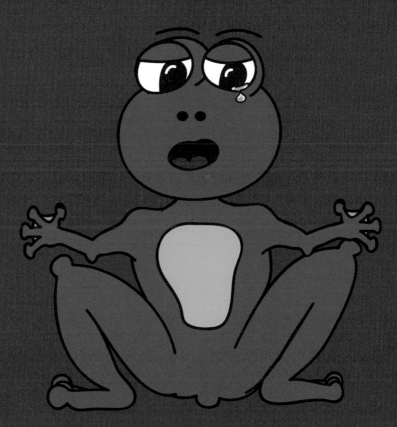

"Is there anything worse
Than a frog who can't croak?
Who **tweets** *when he tries?*
And whose **croaker** *is* **broke**?"

"Now don't be so silly!
Just listen to you.
So you can't go **croak croak!**
Look at what you can do."

"You're a *special* young frog.
There's no one like you.
And that *tweet* that you do—
That's special, too."

Frog took a deep breath
As he dried off his eyes,

Then he **tweet tweeted LOUD!**
What a happy surprise!

And he learned something new
As the days hurried by.
(You never know what
You can do till you try.)

He learned how to **whistle.**
He learned very well.
Now he could whistle
As clear as a bell.

He could whistle some Mozart,
Some Beethoven, too.
He could whistle some jazz,
And his **blues** were real **blue.**

But now I must tell
How my frog story ends.

The boy and the frog
Became very good friends.

They would ride on the hill.
They would ride to beyond.
Then one day, they rode back
To Lily Pad Pond.

And all of the animals
Shouted with joy
When Frog rode to the pond
On the bike with the boy.

*"When you stood on the hill
Could you still see the pond?"*
"How far could you see?"
"Could you see the beyond?"

"**Yes, I could**. I could see it.
And I've been to beyond,
But I'd rather be here
On Lily Pad Pond."

"I'd rather be here
At my home with my friends.
I'd rather be here
Where the winding road ends."

Then Frog started to whistle.
What a beautiful sound!
They thought he was lost,
But now he was found.

His music spreads joy
Wherever he goes.
I knew he could do it.
Now everyone knows.

He's the whistling frog
From Lily Pad Pond.
He has been to the hill
And far, far beyond.

That little green frog
Sure could carry a tune.
I can still almost hear him
From that faraway June.

It was long, long ago—
I was young just like you—
When the whistling frog
Showed us what he could do.

Yes, long, long ago—
I remember him still,
Because I was the boy
From the top of the hill.

And if anyone asks,
Please tell them for me,
The point of my story
Is as plain as can be—

If you don't even try,
You never will know
How great you can be
And how far you can go.